FOR DRACO,
who often gazes at the little white butterflies
in our backyard and once asked me
if they came from our little white flowers . . .

Copyright © 2018 by Danica McKellar

All rights reserved. Published in the United States by Crown Books for Young Readers,
an imprint of Random House Children's Books, a division of Penguin Random House LLC, New York.

Crown and the colophon are registered trademarks of Penguin Random House LLC.

Visit us on the Web! randomhousekids.com

Educators and librarians, for a variety of teaching tools, visit us at RHTeachersLibrarians.com

Library of Congress Cataloging-in-Publication Data is available upon request.
ISBN 978-1-101-93382-4 (trade) —
ISBN 978-1-101-93383-1 (lib. bdg.) —
ISBN 978-1-101-93384-8 (ebook)

The text of this book is set in Carre Noir Demi.
The illustrations were created using pencil and digital paint.

MANUFACTURED IN CHINA
10 9 8 7 6 5 4 3 2
First Edition

DANICA McKELLAR

Ten Magic Butterflies

illustrated by JENNIFER BRICKING

Crown Books for Young Readers ♛ New York

Once upon a time,
there were 10 flower friends.
Were they always happy?
Well, that depends. . . .

All day long,
they soaked up the sun,
talking and laughing
and having fun!

Ha ha ha, hee hee hee!

They loved being flowers . . .
but they couldn't deny
that they had a secret
desire to fly!

They watched every eve
as the fairies flew
from the moonlit night
to the morning dew.

Then, one starry night,
a flower felt brave!
She spotted a fairy
and started to wave.

Said the tiny blue one,
"Fairy up in the sky,
you see, I'm a flower,
but I want to *fly*."

Huh? Oh!

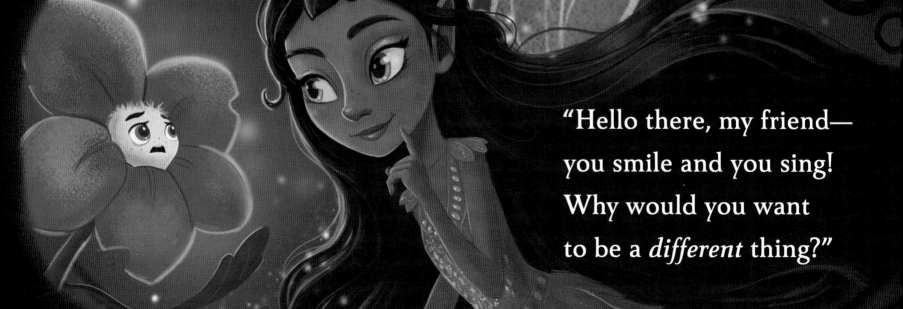

"Hello there, my friend—
you smile and you sing!
Why would you want
to be a *different* thing?"

"I'm tired of being a flower,
just stuck on the ground.
I want new adventures—
to zoom all around!"

The fairy shrugged. "Okay!"
And she closed her eyes.
"Time to get ready
for a big surprise!"

With a wave of her wand
and a **BING BANG BOO!**
the fairy said,
"Now you're a *butterfly*, Blue!"

1 butterfly flew as
9 flowers looked on.
There were still **10** of them—
in the sky, on the lawn.

Said the bossy green one,
"Fairy up in the sky,
hey, make me some wings,
'cause I wanna fly!"

With a wave of her wand
and a BING BANG BOO!

The fairy said,
"Now *you're* a butterfly, too!"

2 butterflies flew as
8 flowers looked on.
There were still **10** of them—
in the sky, on the lawn.

Said the silly orange one,
"Fairy up in the sky,
could I flutter and flip?
Will you help me to fly?"

With a wave of her wand
and a BING BANG BOO!

The fairy said,
"Now *you're* a butterfly, too!"

3 butterflies flew as
7 flowers looked on.
There were still **10** of them—
in the sky, on the lawn.

Next **4** and **6**,

BING BANG BOO!

then **5** and **5**,
the brand-new butterflies
felt alive!

Yes, one by one,
they filled the sky
as the sweet little fairy
helped each to fly.

The **10** new butterflies
flew all night,
zooming and swooping—
what a sight!

Zing, zang, zoom!

When morning came
and the sun peeked through,
their wings were tired
and the wind really blew. . . .

Whoa! Bonk! Thud!

They watched other flowers
soak up the sun
as bees and birds kissed them,
one by one.

RUBBER BAND
★ AIRPLANE ★

And then they said—
together, all 10—
"We actually want
to be flowers again!

"It was fun to fly,
but now we're sad.
We really do miss
all the things we once had. . . ."

Sniff, sniff . . .

"It wasn't bad
when we were flowers. . . ."

"So strong and sturdy
with lots of powers!"

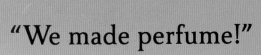

"We made perfume!"

"And cleaned the air!"

"Gave plenty of nectar
for all to share . . ."

"I thought you'd change
your mind!" she cried.
"The grass is always greener
on the other side.

"Sometimes we wish
for different things—
to change color or size,
or even get wings. . . .

"But big and tall,
or short and small,
being ourselves
is best of all!

"So let's go back
to you being *you*
with fairy dust and a

BING BANG BOO!"

Yippee!

Then

10

9

8 7

6 5

4

they floated down
to the garden floor.

Now **7** on the ground
and **3** to go.

Then

3

2

1

zoomed high to low!

Was that a dream?
Or did they fly?
Can flowers end up
with wings in the sky?

Who knows what happens
while we're asleep!
Could dogs become horses
and bugs become sheep?

Neigh? Baaa?

Yes, magic surrounds us.
It takes many forms:
from rainbows and moonlight
to tropical storms.
Frogs come from tadpoles
that swim in the stream.
And each night *you* grow
with every dream. . . .

Shhhh . . .

So don't be surprised
if this story is true
and magical butterflies
come to see you. . . .

You might see one fluttering
late, late at night,
or
in
your
dreams . . .
sleep tight!

Dear Parent/Grandparent/Caregiver,

Congratulations on putting your child on the path to a lifelong love of numbers!

As you probably know, there is an epidemic in this country of kids growing up learning to fear math, which of course can adversely affect their futures in countless ways. It's a slow but steady process that begins at a very young age as they absorb the negative stereotypes surrounding math (that it's foreign, scary, not needed in life) from the media—and even from family and friends. And with every day that passes in our increasingly tech-driven society, math becomes more and more critical for our children's success.

The good news is, we have the power to do something about it! And what is the solution? Making sure our kids see math as "friendly" and *relevant in their lives,* and it's never too soon to start.

In Ten Magic Butterflies, as your child is swept up in the magical transformation of the flowers (and perhaps even absorbing a "grass is always greener" lesson of gratitude!), a very important mathematical concept is on display: "Making 10 in Different Ways," a fundamental stepping-stone to addition and subtraction, and the key to the most important Fact Families they will learn—those totaling 10. Being familiar with this book will also prime your child for the concept of *regrouping,* which will eventually allow him/her to intuitively transform 8 + 5 into 10 + 3 to get the answer 13—no guessing or memorization needed. What a gift! By reading this book every night, we are giving our children tools to excel and are deliberately shaping *how they see math:* as an approachable, integral part of their world.

So when you're at the grocery store, point out the unit prices. When you cook, talk about the fractions on the measuring cups. And when it's time for bed, read books like this one, where I've snuck math education into a story that feels like playtime. You'll be giving your child the priceless gift of confidence in math, helping to shape how the next generation of children see themselves their entire lives—as strong, empowered citizens who understand the value of numbers . . . and who certainly aren't going to let a little math scare them off.

How to get the most out of Ten Magic Butterflies!

- Count the flowers and butterflies out loud on each page, and talk about why the total is always 10. (We aren't gaining or losing any amount when the flowers transform—they are just changing shape!)

- On the endpapers, take note of the flower/butterfly groupings and notice there is always a total of 10. These groupings actually resemble "ten-frames"—a teaching tool your child will see in early elementary school. Ask your child if she/he can tell you how many in each grouping are flowers and how many are butterflies.

- Use your fingers to show how 3 and 7 make 10, how 4 and 6 also make 10, etc.

- Make your own ten-frames at home! Use an egg carton with two sections cut off (so there are 10 instead of 12), and use two different-colored balls or two types of objects to fill them—or even make your own small flowers and butterflies as crafts to fill them. Ask your child which is his/her favorite combination of numbers to make 10.

- Come up with your own ideas, and send them to me at share@McKellarMath.com.

HAPPY COUNTING!